The Secret of Ella and Bloom.

Amberetta Goldheart.

Contents.

Page number

To my best friend Rachel Love Amber x

Letter from the author

Hi guys Amber here and I just want to say a huge thank you for reading this book. This story is personal to me and I'm excited to share it with you guys! I have been writing it for a few years now and kept promising to release it but never got the time and went through a big change in my life and finally got back into writing it. It has been making me feel really happy and the story has become a big part of my life. Some days I would just sit down at my computer hours on end and just type. I hope you can feel close to the characters like I did and I even personally have a favorite if you can figure out who it is then that would be great and see if you find your own.
Enjoy figuring out the secret.
Love Amberetta Goldheart

Ella's side.

Chapter 1: Surprise, surprise!

As soon as I saw him, my heart skipped a beat. I never thought I would fall in love with someone so far away yet so close to my heart. If you really want to hear about how we met, you'll probably want to know who I am, let's begin…

My name is Eloise, but you can call me Ella I am 15 ¼…

That's it really, I'm not as interesting as you would have liked, well make that into, I wasn't as interesting as I thought.

Shall I continue? I will anyway...

It all started when I was walking home with, (how can I put this in a nice way?) a nut case of a friend Sydney Bloom. She wasn't the same walking home because Bloom was quiet. She is never normally this quiet, so I looked at her, and she looked worried, so I asked her calmly;

"What's up, you look upset?" She turned to look at me with such a confused expression on her face. It was like she didn't even know who I was, so I knew something was up. After about 2 minutes she finally took a deep breath and sighed, then whispered: "I don't know why but I joined a teen dating site because looking for a boyfriend where we come from is difficult, so I decided it was better to join this site." Then, putting her hand deep in her pocket, she picked out her phone and showed me the website. Suddenly it all came back to me, a few years back I joined that same site but then forgot completely about it, I replied with a sympathetic smile and looked in her eyes, "There's nothing to be ashamed of. I joined that site a few years ago, it is a really nice website, I will add you on it and we could chat on there, what do you think?" Bloom's eyes lit up, she was so overjoyed but somehow managed to reply with a nod.

When I got home I asked my mum if I could go on the laptop to do some homework, since I got geography homework that day and thought I might as well do it. After being on the computer for an hour, I remember what Bloom said about the website and thought, 'I might as well go on that website since I promised Bloom.' I forgot my password which was annoying, but there's always that button you can press to change your password, so after all the hassle of putting my email in and all the boring details, I finally logged in. Out of the blue, I got a friend request off Bloom and I started laughing hysterically at the fact it said, "Bloom thinks you're a match" which we obviously weren't, just best mates and couldn't imagine us anything else.

After I spoke to Bloom for over an hour, I had an urge to go on webcam since I had a feeling I knew something or someone was on there that I had to see what it was all about. Wait! What am I doing? Suddenly I was on webcam with the cutest boy ever. Looking at him and seeing him look at me back! I needed advice and pronto! I decided to call Bloom because I knew even if she was asleep (even in a deep sleep!) she will pick up anyway because she is my best friend!

Just kidding!

The real reason she picks up is that she always seems to say, "Someone could be calling me about free ice cream, I can not answer, can I?" Weird, right? Anyway...

I called her and after about 7 rings she answered though she sounded so tired and half asleep I had no option but to just have a little giggle to myself. I put myself on mute and just smiled and went out the room. "BLOOM!!! There's a cute guy on webcam and we just keep looking at each other I don't know should I stay on or just go because it's so awkward no one's speaking!!" Bloom just burst into laughter, so I had to wait forever and a day for her to calm down. The good thing about her is that even though Bloom can be a joker when you want her to be serious and have a grown-up conversation with her, she will be so serious it's scary! Mainly because she's the oldest and gives out the most amazing advice anyone can give.

Finally, she replied, "Listen if you want to speak the best way is to say hi and to then ask him: 'How are you?', 'How's your day been?', 'What have you done?' and so on because once you start a conversation it will take forever to stop." It sounds simple, right?

WRONG! Even saying 'hi' takes a lot of courage and that's the one thing that scares me.

I took a deep breath and decided instead of saying it out loud I would just ask for his number and message him as it wouldn't be as awkward. I left the webcam conversation and decided to message.

We started to message and then we couldn't stop talking. It was like he was a boy version of me it was unbelievable.

A few days past and unlike other friendships on this site, we just kept talking. After about a week he asked me to be his girlfriend so of course, I said YES with no hesitation. No one could stop us from talking, or so we thought.

Chapter 2: The meet up.

After a few weeks, we decided we should meet up; we calculated the distance from mine to his and found out it was big. In the end the nearest place to me was a mall that was 30 minutes away from where I live but sadly it was an hour or two away from where he lived but he promised it didn't even matter to him, but even after he said that I still felt guilty that he had to get his parents to drive him for up to two hours just to see me.

Sadly, the date kept changing because both his parents were working on the days we choose so after about a month the final date we chose was a success! His parents were off, and he was free, I was so excited that I would be able to meet him in person and not just on a computer screen. I couldn't hold the joy inside I had to call Bloom straight away.

"Oh, my gosh Bloom! Today's the day I can't wait! Are you still coming with me? Please say you are?" Bloom was as excited as I was because she wanted to see

Shaun (my new boyfriend) in person but most importantly, she couldn't wait to see me happy. It was a bit risky since we hadn't met in person before we had only seen each other on webcam and FaceTime so Bloom wanted to make sure I was safe. She replied "Yes, of course, I am coming I wouldn't miss this for the world! I am one of your best mates I want you to be happy!" But I secretly knew that she was coming to protect me and make sure he is who he said he was, and that I can never go alone to meet a stranger. She even made sure the time was set so that the mall will be packed, making sure we met in a big public area full of people. Bloom didn't want to be boring so tried to make sure it was a fun place, so in the middle of Selfridges near the shoes was the best place, which I also agreed on although it was a bit random. Don't you agree?

Anyway…

I was finally ready and waiting for Bloom. (She is always a few minutes late, so I get used to it.) She turned up to mine 20 minutes late, no surprise. She came to my door and for once she looked fashionable.

She was wearing a sky blue colored baggy top with knee high ivory leggings' and leather black knee-high boots (no heel).

I was wearing my high waisted blue jeans, blue tank top, and red converse. (Since it was Shaun's' favorite outfit on me.)

I wouldn't change my style for anyone, so I just chucked on my denim jacket which went with anything and left.

"I am so excited! What if he doesn't like me once he looks at me? What if he thinks that I am not his type anymore?" I was worrying so much I even thought that he would take one look at me and decide that I am not worth it anymore. I didn't even notice Bloom was out of breath. She had run from the wrong metro stop that was far away from my house when she could have got off at the next stop which was just around the corner, although she does always forget about that one.

Bloom rudely interrupted me and stated: "If he doesn't like you then why would he be meeting you? It is not about the image it is mostly about your personality and who you are not what you look like. Trust me you're pretty and gorgeous; If I was a boy I know you would be on my "who to date list" since your kind, honest and an all-around nutter. Any boy would be blind not to notice your beauty and a normal boy would be jealous of any boy on your arm."

When Bloom had finished her rant I still had a little doubt, but if I didn't go I would've never known how he really felt about me.

We decided we would get the first bus that came and take it to the big bus stop so then we could get a bus straight from there to the mall, so we could get there quicker.

OH, NO got to the bus stop and saw the bus wouldn't come for another 20 minutes! How can we get there in time? That day couldn't get any worse...

Spoke too soon! Shaun then got stuck in traffic and he wasn't even halfway. I didn't know what was going to happen anymore, will he just leave and go home?

In the end, we decided that if me and Bloom wait for the bus to come whilst he is in traffic we would all end up at the mall at the same time.

Finally, after what it felt like hours waiting the bus came, Bloom then realized that the bus would take more than half an hour to get to the mall so hopefully we would arrive at the same time as Shaun or else I wouldn't have known what to do.

After half an hour of being on the bus with Bloom talking about anything that popped into her head. (She even started talking about her head coming first in a potato competition.) We finally arrived at the mall.

We decided to meet in the middle of Selfridges, but where is the middle of Selfridges? Shaun then texted Bloom that he was next to the toys but Bloom being Bloom walked in the completely wrong direction and ended up in the food section (which isn't all bad) still how we ended up there I will never remember. We spent 10 minutes trying to find our way around to meet him. We all remembered we had chosen to meet near the shoes and we all knew where that was, so we walked over to the shoes.

OH, MY GOSH!!! He was there... Stood at my eye level...

Should I run away and go home? NO, I have been waiting for this day for months, I didn't know what to do I just froze, as still as a statue.

He came rushing over, his arms open ready for me to swoop in and hold him, it was like the world had stopped in a matter of seconds. I was in his loving arms for the first time hoping it won't be the last time. I closed my eyes. My head resting on his shoulder, so comfortable in his presence, it was truly unreal. I never wanted it to end.

Bloom came over and just laughed her head off.

"So, Ella what do you want to do today?" Bloom asked completely forgetting what had just happened because she thought that hugging someone was too cringe.

Chapter 3: When Bloom orders your drink...

After a few hours of walking around and doing nothing I finally asked, "Does anybody want to go to a cafe?" without even replying Bloom scurried off into the nearest cafe, barged past everybody and ordered all our drinks. She didn't even ask us what we wanted, instead just ordered the drinks. Trust Bloom to be random on the first meet up and know what we want.

Shaun just laughed and turned to me, put his mouth to my ear and whispered: "Will you do me the honor and let me kiss you and be yours forever and always?"

I just went red in the face and eyes teary and nodded as if I was saying "Oh, yes please: I am all yours." I felt so embarrassed but as his rosy lips touched mine it was like I was kissing a soft, velvet-like pillow. Why do I suddenly feel this way? We have only just met, this is weird.

I got my Caramel Frappuccino with whip cream and so did Shaun and Bloom.

(Which basically means Bloom ordered three drinks the same.) I wanted to tell Bloom what really happened in the café, what Shaun whispered to me, but I knew she will end up mothering me and I didn't want her to start complaining saying 'you're going too fast, slow down you will end up doing something you will regret!' You might break up and then you will look at this like a sad memory' and so on, so on.

Bloom is my best friend and I have never kept a secret like this, but I didn't want her to overreact, I couldn't decide what was the most loving thing to do, other than to not tell her about what happened.

I loved hanging out in the café with them, my favorite part was when Shaun started chasing Bloom round *the cafe* since Bloom took his phone, she started taking as many selfies as she could. In the end, Shaun ended up having 50 selfies of just Bloom pulling faces towards him.

When I look back at all the events that happened that day, I always go back to what Shaun whispered in my ear. That is when I knew for sure he liked me for who I was, not for what I looked or sounded like.

"Hey, guys! When you think about it, I could go away now and leave you two, since you are getting on so well."- Suggested Bloom. She winked at me, I knew what she was on about, and I didn't want to be alone because I felt I would be shy. I feel like it was my first crush all over again, (you know the crush you get in primary when you finally notice boys aren't from Mars?)
Bloom walked away and went to look at the mall and left me and Shaun alone. At first, it was awkward as no one knew what to say; Shaun then had the courage to say, "I really love you and I never want this day to end!"

Sadly, the day did end. His mum called him and asked him to meet her in the same place she dropped him off. It was heartbreaking to see him leave, but it had to happen this way. I felt so lost without hearing his voice, I got Bloom to call him straight away. Was that too needy? I didn't think so because we are in love.

Chapter 4: What happens when you get back to school with a boyfriend?

Going to school was the hardest part of that week! I got in and Bloom comes rushing up to me screaming "Ella it's horrible! People are asking so many questions about Shaun and I don't know what to answer with!" I didn't even know how to answer Bloom's questions.

Why do relationships have to be so difficult? I thought about it for a bit then, I suddenly felt like there was a weight in my stomach; I missed Shaun. I finally replied with "If they want to know what happened so badly, they can come and ask me in person, not through a messenger, because realistically it is none of their business what has happened really, is it?" I didn't know why I lashed out at Bloom because it wasn't her fault.

"Sorry if I sounded a little harsh and like I'm angry at you because I'm not it is just the pressure of being back at school if you get what I mean?"

Bloom nodded with tears in her eyes since I had a go at her. She then ran off into the toilet, because Bloom is unique and very sensitive as she wants everyone to like her. If they show even a little bit of hatred she will have a moment.

I decided to go off and see everyone else and see what the fuss was about, plus I hadn't seen them in what felt like months ago.

The first person I bumped into was my mate Linsey, as she came running over with joy written all over her face and asked, "So is it true?" and I just blushed and nodded looking so embarrassed. She immediately asked me for all the details, which I couldn't tell her because she wouldn't have understood the concept of how we met, and why we are going out either.

She was the gossip of the school because all she ever did was spread around rumors about people. Half of them weren't even true and the other half she wasn't meant to know anyway.

Many people thought that Linsey was a two-faced liar, but we trusted her anyway. She was our friend, but we learned over time not to tell her anything that was embarrassing, or that we didn't want to be spread around school.

My first lesson went great, but I couldn't get Bloom off my mind. She was too vulnerable. People were going up to her, asking her questions about me and Shaun. It would certainly break her, and she may even spread the secret. As soon as my first lesson was finished I rushed to science, as it was Bloom's second lesson too. If I get there earlier, I may be able to bump into Bloom and ask if she was okay.
Bloom didn't come to science…

The break was after science, so once science was finished, I went looking for Bloom. I found her at a table with her face as pale as a white blank sheet of paper, I wondered what was up.
"Bloom are you okay?" I put my arm around her and let her cry on my shoulder. I wanted to know what was up, but before she could open her mouth to speak, Linsey was there. She started asking her all the questions in the world. Bloom couldn't answer any of them.

I shouted "Just get your filthy nose out of it and go get a bath! If she wanted to tell you what was up, she would have told you in the first place and if she wants to tell you what's up she will in her own time! Now please just go away!"

She may have glared at me, but the thing is, that if I hadn't have said anything she would have made the situation worse and I really needed to talk to Bloom in private.

After Bloom calmed down she said "I can't take it! This secret about you meeting Shaun! I had to say he was my cousin's best mate, and that you met him at a New Year's Eve party at my house. I have never lied to people so close to me before."

I felt bad for Bloom, but I was happy that she could tell people about how we met him. Even though it was a lie, I was happy that she was so loyal to me. I hugged her so tight I felt like I was suffocating her, but it was worth it. I felt I could say thanks to her for being there for me no matter what.

"Bloom, just remember that whatever happens, we will be there for each other. But now I need you to do a massive favor for me." I was scared that she would say no for doing this favor. However, she said: "Sure, anything for you Ella. What is it?" and so I said: "When me and Shaun say how we really met. Will you stand by my side and not let anyone say, 'we shouldn't have done it because, at the time, we felt that it was right? Just promise me you will never leave me!" As soon as I said this she came up and hugged me. Whispered in my ear "We are together forever and always I will never leave you to be on your own. Even if we fall out and completely hate each other, I will never tell anyone what actually happened that night!"

Chapter 5: The secret about the ring

It has been a while since I have met Shaun. So much has happened between me and Bloom. We have become close and we even do a movie night, in which Shaun and us, go and watch a movie together just for the fun of it.

The last time we did a movie night, we just got bored and decided to look at what new movies were out. 'Fifty Shades of Grey' was the first thing that came up, and we all looked at each other and said: "Why not? Let's watch it!"

"Err mm Ella, why are we watching this?" Asked Bloom because she didn't know what was going on. Before I could answer Bloom's, question Shaun answered comically "we are coming up to the best part!" whilst the main characters were negotiating contracts. I just laughed and so did Bloom.

At the end of the movie, Shaun needed to ask me a question, and I didn't know what was going on, so Bloom giggled and said, "I'm just going to the toilet, stay here for a minute."

But whilst Bloom was gone Shaun went on one knee and said "This is a promise ring, it promises me that no matter what, we will always be together. That when we are older we will one day get married, just not yet as we are still young." He showed me this infinity ring which was jeweled, and I just smiled.

Then a flashback swept through my mind...

It was about a month before Bloom came rushing up to me asking, "OMG Ella what is your ring size? I need to know for.... errrmmm.... a science experiment?" I just looked at her with a confused expression and answered. "I don't know mine! Want to go to the ring shop tonight and measure our ring fingers?" Bloom nodded and rushed off on the phone to someone, but I didn't know at the time that Shaun was responsible for planning this. We then rushed off after school to the ring shop. We then looked at rings and tried loads on. I made Bloom ask the shop assistant about measuring our ring fingers, and the shop assistant just laughed and said, "Sure as long as none of you two are getting married, you look too young!"- She said this in a jokey way, so we just looked at her with a confused expression because at the time we didn't understand the joke.

We found out our ring sizes. We decided that maybe one day we would go back there, when we really are getting married to try on wedding rings again, and then make sure it would be even more memorable.

Unaware that whilst this was going on, Bloom texted Shaun the ring sizes to which, he replied "OK. Ask her that if she was to have any ring, what ring would it be?" I had no clue why Bloom was asking these questions at the time, but now I understand. It was so out of the blue how this all happened, but I enjoyed every moment.

After Shaun presented the ring, I felt like my heart was going to explode! He looked like he was happy to be with me. Like I was his whole world. I didn't know if I wanted this to happen or not, but I said: "Yes, you're my whole world!"- And hugged him extremely tight. Suddenly I did not want to let go; he was mine. If I let him go, then that would be me giving him away... I would never do that to someone so precious and close to my heart.

He seemed to be aware of my emotions and whispered: "I know you never want to let me go, but Bloom's staring at us!" I looked over and Bloom was giggling with happiness. She knew all along and looked extremely proud of me for saying the magical 'yes'.

I never knew where Bloom went after that, but me and Shaun decided to go back to mine for a bit. Once back at mine we waited for Shaun's parents to pick him up, deep down I wished they would never come, but I knew the sooner he was gone the sooner he would come back.

When Shaun's' parents came to pick him up, I immediately got on my phone and called Bloom.
"Oh my gosh Bloom it was the best day ever! When can we do something like this again?"
There was a pause…
"Ella, I think it is best if you go and see him on your own next time."
Bloom has never said that to me before so maybe she's right, next time I will go on my own and then maybe something might happen between us. I do love him and have never felt like this towards someone before, I can't wait and see what we do next.

Chapter 6: What happens next?

It feels like forever since I have spoken to Shaun, the last memory of that day was when he walked me to the door, held me and said he would talk to me when he got home.

But I cried, not only because I missed him but because I was terrified. I was terrified I was going to fall in love, terrified he would be the one then leaves me but mostly terrified he loves me the same way. I've never felt this way about anyone before and at first, I didn't know if it was love or a crush again, but after that day I knew that I was very much in love with him, I felt broken when he wasn't there, I knew I would see him again and I was just meant to wait for the next time I could see him again.

It was not until a few months later that we would see each other again but that was due to one thing…
Isaac.
Isaac, I couldn't find one nice thing about Isaac, he nearly ruined everything between me and Shaun.

Isaac was also good friends with Cody, I thought Cody would try and sway Isaac to be nicer about mine and Shaun's relationship, but Isaac kept a grudge against the relationship, but I could never understand why, or even imagine why. Still, to this day I can't figure anything out but the day I first met him I could see it.

The hatred…

It all started when I went over to see Shaun in his hometown with Bloom, it was scary at first, but I thought to myself if I didn't see him then it would be forever till I see him again. We took the train as it was a very long journey to his school. Bloom was so excited that we ended up sitting in first class as she was disturbing the other passengers in the business class, (was annoying at first but we got upgraded thanks, Bloom!) She was shouting "I can't wait to see everyone! Are you excited because I am?" To everyone, even people she hasn't seen before in her life. I just laughed and said, "Yes I am excited now calm down before we get sent off." We ended up getting told by the ticket inspector to move to first class as no one's in there to annoy. When we got to

Shaun's town we were an hour early, so Bloom suggested something stupid. She suggested to go to the supermarket and get donuts. I know it doesn't sound that stupid, but you will see in a bit what I mean. When I look back at it now, I see how stupid it was.

We got into the supermarket and Bloom immediately found the doughnuts at the back of the shop, she knew where the bakery was without asking anyone, even though she has never been there before in her life. She decided to buy a big bottle of sparkly flavored water with a packet of small doughnuts with chocolate sauce. (Big mistake!) I decided to buy myself a strawberry flavored drink with a small packet of biscuits, as I didn't want food around my mouth when I meet Shaun. When we got to his school, which was a 15-minute walk up a small hill, Bloom decided to open her doughnuts and ate 2 before we even got to the top of the hill.
We saw Shaun as soon as we got to his school and he opened his arm, so I couldn't help myself but run into them and hug him tightly. Bloom was too busy eating the doughnuts to notice we were with Shaun, she looked up,

but she didn't see us first… she saw Isaac. He looked at me then at Bloom and said, "Who are those two?"
Bloom just froze as still as a statue, she has instincts that predict if someone is nice or horrible, her reaction to Isaac was immediate alarm bells. The whole day he was glaring at me and Bloom and it made us feel uneasy, Bloom turned to me and whispered in my ear, "Please get Shaun to get rid of Isaac he is making me feel like I've done something wrong, all he is doing is glaring. Can we go?"
I looked over at Shaun and lied. Right to his face.
"Shaun me and Bloom have to go, our train is due now sorry." And left.

That night Shaun was calling me, he just kept asking why I left in such a hurry and if he was to blame but of course he wasn't but I couldn't explain it in a way that wouldn't offend him nor his friend. I had to say "I will tell you the truth, it wasn't you, it was Bloom. She was feeling uncomfortable around Isaac, he was glaring the whole time at us was something up?"
Shaun was silent.

"Shaun? You still there?" Suddenly there was a loud sigh. Shaun then replied, "I am here but why do you care so much about Bloom? If she felt so bad about the situation, why didn't you tell her to leave and stayed with me? I am more important as I am your boyfriend!" Then hung up.

Silence.

The whole room was silent. I couldn't cry, I couldn't scream, I was motionless. That was the first time he had said something so mean about Bloom. I didn't know what to say and I certainly did not know what to do next.

Chapter 7: The secret is out.

The morning came really slowly as the argument ended up lasting until 1 am. Sadly it ended with me turning my phone off and falling asleep, I just couldn't handle the thought of arguing over something so little, I then decided we needed space to think things through and see how things are.

I then got ready for school although I definitely was not in the mood to go, people would ask me millions of questions about how me and Shaun are doing. I turned my phone on to message Bloom that I would be late and to go to school on her own, I then looked and just that morning I had 12 missed calls from her but just as I was about to message her to explain, she called me. "Oh, my gosh Ella, Shaun messaged me last night asking how you were doing and why you weren't answering the phone. I then said you might have just fallen asleep, but he then started saying you blamed me for us going early and I was confused can you explain?" My heart sank, she was on the verge of crying, her voice was breaking and sounding like she was holding back the tears, I just couldn't reply when she was in that state. I didn't even know what to say because I don't want to hurt her feelings and say she was a bit sensitive, but I would hate to lie, and it gets back to Shaun. In the end, I decided to just hang up.

Before you say anything, I know I shouldn't have hung up, if you were in my position you may have done the same thing. I to this day still feel bad about it but just listening to Bloom's voice and knowing that she is probably going to cry just made my heart die a little inside.

There was a sudden banging at the door. Why couldn't I move to answer it? I was still and scared no one was meant to be coming over, it was 8 o'clock in the morning and the post doesn't come till 10 so it wasn't the postman who was it?

"Ella please answer the door! I need to talk to you, it is important, and I can't hold it back any longer!" It was Bloom… Why is she here? What does she want to tell me? I was so confused but inside I knew I wouldn't find out just standing in the corridor, the door needed to be opened and I was the only one who could do it.

I walked slowly over to get the key, I was shaking like crazy, and I secretly didn't want to know in case it was something I couldn't have control over. Could it be something to do with Shaun? Who cares right now

Bloom sounded like she needed me, and I needed her. I put the key in the door, turned it clockwise and opened the door.

Bloom stood there, drenched from head to foot as she didn't have a coat on only her blazer and school uniform. She looked like she couldn't stop crying, but the question that was stuck in my mind was why?
"Ella I'm sorry, everyone at school knows how you met Shaun. Last night when your phone was off Shaun was posting about how much he loves you and he posted this." She unlocked my phone and showed me an Instagram picture of me and Shaun that he posted which had a massive comment which read; "This girl is my world I wouldn't want to spend the rest of my life with anyone else. From the day we met online, and I looked at her and she looked at me, that day I knew who I wanted and loved."

I was speechless. Why did he do this? Yes, I admit it was a kind thought and means well but now I must go to school and deal with people asking me questions. Bloom looked at me and asked, "What do you want to do?" I had no response, I wasn't sure myself on what I wanted to do.

I left it a minute, did a deep sigh and replied. "Honestly Bloom I have no clue, what do I do now? I might just go to school and ignore everyone's' questions about me and Shaun."

And I did.

It was very stressful every lesson I would hear, "What website was it?", "Did you only go on it for attention?", "Have you broken up with him?" etc.

I just went from lesson to lesson holding my head down, wouldn't make eye contact with anyone. Then went home.

As soon as I got home I cried, not the usual cry out loud for everyone to hear, no it was different. I went upstairs, sat on my bed and just cried. No noise, no movement, just tears falling down my face. I felt like my world was going wrong, but I had no control over what was happening.

I needed to get my mind off what was happening, the only thing I could think about was Bloom. I didn't know if she wanted to speak to me or not after me ignoring her for the whole day, but if I didn't speak to her I don't think I can survive the night. I decided I should call her and talk to her about how I am feeling and if she has any suggestions about what I should do.

I rang her... She didn't pick up. So I decided to try again, but still no answer. What's going on?

Right, so I can't tell you how long it was till she answered the phone, but this is how it went. You probably are wondering what the story is about what the secret is, and why Bloom wasn't answering the phone right?

Well, I'm sorry but you will have to keep reading to find out because I can't explain it right now as I doubt Bloom would let me say it this soon in the story.

Well I finally got in contact with Bloom and I figured out her secret, but she didn't know. I was so shocked, why didn't she trust me enough to tell me something as big as this? Then again, I understood what she was going through, I emphasized with her and wanted her to feel comfortable, but I couldn't tell her I knew as it just wouldn't feel right, how would I explain that I found her secret out. I don't want you to feel like I am writing a completely new story, but this is the only way I can explain to you guys how I found out about Bloom, it happens to be the night I was crying in my bedroom over Shaun. I won't tell you what the secret was, I'll let you figure out the secret for yourselves.

So I will explain how I found it out let's begin...

"Bloom finally you answer I am so sorry... Bloom, are you crying?" Bloom was sniffling I could hear her try and keep the tears down, I had no idea what happened, was it my fault? I swear I never meant to hurt her in any way. Luckily she said "It isn't you, just me and Rosie... Never mind you won't know what I am on about."

What Bloom didn't know was that I actually did know who Rosie was. "Bloom, look I do know who Rosie is. She is your best friend from outside school." Bloom was silent, I kept saying "Hello?" Still no reply. I took the phone from my cheek, wiped the foundation stain off the screen, and then placed it back on my ear. "Bloom? You still there? Hello?" I heard a loud sigh and then she replied with, "Yes she is my best friend from outside school, we had an argument, but it will be fine, how are you feeling after today?"

I could sense she was trying to change the subject, I had to go with it and answer what she was asking with no questions.

In a way, I replied saying that everything was okay but I knew that if I spoke to Shaun we could work everything out, but Blooms my best mate so I wanted to get to the bottom of everything and figure out what was going on inside her head.

Chapter 8: Friends are forever.

I spent the night on the phone with Shaun and we sorted everything out. He decided that he put the message on his Instagram because he didn't want to keep his love and how we met a secret because he loved me. Plus he wasn't really thinking about what he was typing anyway which I laughed about.

But for most of the conversation, we were talking about Bloom. Shaun was saying "Ella I am truly sorry for what happened, I never meant to hurt your feelings but may I ask what is up with Bloom? She hasn't posted on her snapshat, Instagram or even her Facebook? And she has been ghosting me, just looking at my messages and not replying, are you two okay?"

I didn't know what to say, I couldn't reveal what is going on with her because I wasn't 100% sure myself. So I took a deep breath and said "Honestly I have no clue, she has had an argument with one of her best friends from outside school and she took it to heart and was so upset so I just want to be there for her so I am really truly happy about us two making up." I then went on to explain what I thought was going on but couldn't tell him the big secret because he would tell people, I know we are meant to be close and not keep secrets, but this isn't my secret to tell. Let's be honest if I told anyone this secret my friendship with Bloom will just break up, and I would lose my best friend ever. I believe the friendship is built on this secret and if I didn't keep this secret bloom wouldn't trust anyone ever again.

Shaun agreed that something weird was definitely up with Bloom and that Shaun and I should just makeup and pretend that everything is okay between us and to focus all the energy on making sure Bloom is happy and okay.

Shaun messaged Bloom that night saying "Bloom I know that you are upset and that something may be going on in your life but trust me things do get better and a problem shared is a problem halved. You have me and Ella to talk to if you need to, we are here for you just message us."

Bloom looked at the message but didn't reply so I got worried, she hardly ever doesn't reply if someone is messaging her, what is going on? I called her…

"Bloom, oh Bloom just please answer me." After ringing around 3 times she picked up.

"Hi, Ella what's up?" She sounded okay but I knew she was hiding something from me as she would usually answer the phone straight away, so I decided I would be straight with her.

"Bloom I know something is up with you, it wouldn't take you this long to answer the phone. Have you done something that you think I would be mad at? Have you had another argument? Please just tell me I promise you I won't be mad." She just started crying really loudly and I decided to go round to hers.

"That's it, Bloom, I will be over in 15 minutes!" I ran out of the house straight away.

It isn't that far from my house to the met so I ran, got on the first met that came and went to Blooms. As me and Bloom have been friends since, like, forever it made it easier for me to just walk into her house and run quickly up to her bedroom, where I saw what looked like a heartbroken Bloom, with red bloodshot eyes, sat on her floor with her phone in her hand. This made it look to me like she had been crying for days none stop, so I saw it as my duty as one of her best friends to find, and figure out what was up to then solve it.

"Bloom!" I ran over and sat on the floor next to her then gave her the biggest and softest hug in the world and stayed like that to say, "I know you are hurting and it is my responsibility to find what has hurt you and solve it. Now please no more secrets between us what is going on?"

Bloom pushed me back so I would stop hugging her, walked over to her bed and sat crossed legged and started telling me.

"Ella comes sit next to me I need to tell you something." She said this whilst patting the space next to her so I would walk over and sit next to her, she placed her hands on top of mine and told me everything from the start to the end about what was happening in her life, and reasons why she had been acting the way she was. This made me well-up, then whilst I wiped away some tears I mumbled; "Bloom, you know you could have told me what was happening, and why did Rosie not help you? She was meant to be your best friend and you know that if you couldn't go to me, you should have gone to Rosie."

Then Bloom explained that Rosie was mostly the problem and how she couldn't tell me in full detail now but she will once she has found a solution.

"You see Ella my life is way too complicated, but I feel like I should tell you a secret I have been keeping to myself for way too long." She takes a deep breath holds back the tears and whispers it into my ear.

"Oh my Bloom, I don't know what to say. I am really happy for you. Can I just say one thing though?"

She looked me in the eyes, still crying and went; "Yes what is it?"

"Ella I have to say that I did figure that secret out a couple of days ago, but I just felt it right for you to tell me yourself instead of me assuming, but I never expected Rosie to be such a big part."

The rest of the night was just me and Bloom talking and figuring out what to do next and with such a big secret resting on my shoulders as well as Blooms, it made Bloom feel relieved and like she could turn to me whenever she needed someone to talk to.

I ended up staying the night as it was a Friday and we luckily had nothing on the next day, plus her parents didn't mind and Bloom felt like I was a part of the family anyway.

Chapter 9: Who is Rosie?

Throughout this story, I have always been going on about Rosie and Bloom's friendship but never really mentioned the full backstory of who Rosie is and what her friendship with Bloom was. I believe that when it is Bloom's turn to tell the story she will mention more about who Rosie is and what she understands about the friendship but I will say what I know.

When I was sat on Blooms bed the next day I went on my phone and to message Shaun about what happened that night, but for some reason I didn't know how to explain it without spilling the secret plus I didn't know that much about who Rosie is and what connection she has with Bloom so I decided to ask Bloom myself.

"Bloom I need to ask you something and it's kind of important." I looked up from my phone and looked over to Bloom who was on her laptop, she turned around stared at me and said, "Yes what's up?" I sighed walked over, sat down next to her on the floor and asked "The thing is I have been thinking about it, what we spoke about last night, and don't really know who Rosie is. Can you please tell me who she is, only if you feel up to it?" Bloom was speechless, she looked at me and turned around and went on her computer. At first, I was like, she is being really rude and ignoring the question but then I thought, she can't be ignoring me she usually answers the question straight away. After about 3 minutes of silence, Bloom said, "Ella come over here, this is who Rosie is."
She showed me a picture of a sort brown haired girl with skin as white as snow, she wore black squared glasses and the greenest eyes I have ever seen. Have you ever

seen grass in the summer? Where the grass is bright green and fresh like emeralds? Well, that was the sort of eyes Rosie had.

Though I have never seen this girl around my area and I usually know who everyone is, this is only because we live in a small area and it is the sort of place where everyone knows everyone's business and problems.

I decided to do some investigating myself I left Blooms gave her a massive hug and said: "Don't let anyone bring you down, just know I love you and if you ever need me I am only a phone call away." And went home.

When I got home I went over to my bedroom sat on my bed and called Shaun. "Shaun right here's the deal, whilst at Blooms, I asked who Rosie is and she showed me a picture and told me the story of how they met."

Bloom did tell me the story of how they met but I am sure she will write down that part of her story herself and explain it to you.

Shaun replied after a few minutes of taking it in with, "Right so you have never seen this girl but know what she looks like, can't you find her on Bloom's Facebook?"

So I grabbed my laptop, opened it up and searched Blooms Facebook friends for someone called Rosie, and it came up straight away. I looked through her pictures and there were loads of her and Bloom, and they looked really happy next to one another.

I then looked at what school she went to and immediately recognized it, The Amber Academy of Performing Arts, it was half an hour on a train down so it wasn't that far but it still confused me how they... wait I know. I figured it out why didn't I notice it before.

"Shaun I have looked through her Facebook and Rosie goes to your school! She is only a year below you, I'll send you a picture from her Facebook see if you recognize her, I'm sure you would." I heard Shaun open his laptop and look at the picture I sent him on the Facebook messenger. "Oh my Ella, I have seen her around before she does go to my school!"

Shaun lives the same distance away from me as Rosie lives away from Bloom so when I thought about how they met, Bloom must have gone through Shaun's

Facebook and found Rosie and messaged her. That's the only thing logical I could think of.

"Shaun do you think you could speak to Rosie on Monday, ask her questions, but not too many as we don't want to make her feel uncomfortable." Shaun agreed, and we spoke late into the night about what we think we should speak about and what sort of things we want to know about Rosie. Then fell asleep on the phone.

I think that's all I can tell you about the secret. Have you figured it out yet? Hope not as there is more to the story than you may believe. I have kept loads of things from you guys but only because I think Bloom has more to say than me. So I will let you guys guess and make assumptions but by the end of this book, I'm sure you will understand why we kept it a secret for this long.

Talk to you guys later.
Ella xx

Bloom's side.

Chapter 10: Bloom.

Hey, it's bloom. I've decided that after reading Ella's interpretation of the secret, I myself should tell you my side of the story and may even mention what the secret is, so here I go.

That day when Ella saw me upset walking home from school, I kind of didn't tell her the full truth about the dating site, the thing was, I wasn't looking for a boyfriend, I was, in fact, looking for a new best friend, this was going to hurt Ella's feeling and that was not the intention. I wanted someone I could talk to outside of school and tell them my problems, this is because and I didn't know how to tell her, without me feeling she would be mad at me. I also felt that I was a burden on Ella, which is why I feel that all my problems are kept inside now and it does hurt.

I started to freak out as she kept asking me what was up, I just stared at her I couldn't explain what was going on, and she might not understand.so after about two minutes I sighed and told her that I joined a dating site but when I found out she was on it too I was over the moon.

When she told me "I will add you to it and we could chat on there, what do you think?" I felt really happy because it would be something we could do together, so I nodded and went home. When I got home I went straight into my room, sat at my table and went on my laptop. I logged into the dating site and searched for Blooms name, I found her and sent her a request, but then I noticed a girl called Rosie was online, I thought about it for a minute and decided that I would look at her profile and see if she would be okay to be my new friend.
At first, I didn't like the look of her as she was a bit plain compared to me. As you probably know my fashion is more outgoing and I do try to be a fashionista, but then it just goes south.

I decided why not message her, just a simple message like, "Hi, how are you? Doing anything fun today?" Just little questions to start a conversation, because who knows she may not even reply. So, I sent off a little message, then decided to pop up to Ella and see how she is doing, maybe even message her about our maths homework because it was very hard algebra. I spoke to Ella for about an hour then checked my messages, I had a message from Rosie.

I froze for a moment, why was she messaging me back? She must have thought I was nice to talk to, or she could have liked the look of me.

Anyway, I read her reply; "Hi Bloom, I am good just finished doing my homework for school. It was really hard but I can just relax now. How are you? I think you look really nice to talk to, hope we could be friends."

Yes! I want to be her friend, I sound very upfront and extremely enthusiastic even though she is still a stranger, and you shouldn't just be friends with strangers. I kept messaging her and we really got along, we spoke till very late then I got a call from Ella. Why is she calling me this late? I will answer and see if everything is okay, plus she may be calling me because it might be free ice cream.

"Ella is everything okay?" I acted really tired because if I acted awake she would be asking me questions about why I am up so late, I couldn't tell her the truth, could I? She started going on about a cute guy she saw on webcam and how she really liked him but no one was talking. I agree it does sound awkward. As it was awkward I started laughing, every time something gets awkward I start to laugh because it's my way of coping. After I had finished I decided to give her advice, I knew this advice would work as I did the same thing with Rosie; "Listen if you want to speak the best way is to say hi and to then ask him: 'How are you?', 'How's your day been?', 'What have you done?', and so on because once you start a conversation it will take forever to stop." I thought about what I said for a second, it must work as I asked Rosie similar questions, after I said the advice to Ella she thanked me and hung up. I gave a big sigh walked over to my bed and jumped on it, picked up my phone, thought about replying to people, but I was too tired so I fell asleep.

After a few days I was getting really close with Rosie, we spoke every day, added each other to all the social media we had and decided to be each other's best friends. I had also then found out that Ella was getting close with Shaun, speaking about the same amount as me and Rosie. I still never told her about Rosie though, I didn't feel a need to.

Until the day Rosie asked me to meet her…

Chapter 11: The two meet ups in a day.

When I was walking home Ella came running up behind me, I had to quickly put my phone into my blazer pocket as I was messaging Rosie and still wasn't ready to tell her about what was happening. "Bloom I'm so glad I caught up with you, I am just wondering if you are available on Saturday? As Shaun wanted to meet up with me and I need you to come along?" I thought about it for a second because I didn't really know this Shaun fella, and that was, to me, a reason to go. "Yes, I will come, this is to make sure that you are safe and nothing bad will happen to you." The joy on Ella's face was just the reply I needed, it was indescribable. She was so happy, it was like her grin could go on for days. I hugged her and whispered in her ear; "You do know that you don't have to be this happy, you haven't won the lottery just yet." We laughed and walked to the met stop and took the met home.

I got home and went straight to my room, sat at my desk and opened my laptop up. I went onto my Facebook and wrote Rosie a message; 'Sorry for a late reply my phone ran out of battery, what are you doing on Saturday? I am asking as I am going to a mall that is near me and wondering after going out with Ella and Shaun if you wanted to meet me at mine and hang out? You could even sleepover I am sure my mum wouldn't mind?' and sent it.

Saturday came sooner than we had expected, I had tidied my room the night before and got my spare bed down from the loft, mum allowed Rosie to come over in one condition, that condition was that my dad and me go and pick her up from her house, so my dad can meet Rosie's parents. I didn't mind this condition because it means that Rosie can stay, and my parents can now meet my new best friend, I was so excited!

I got ready wearing a comfy sky blue top, I made sure it was baggy as it would allow me to be comfy on the ride to Rosie's house after I had been to the mall. I also wore my favorite Ivory leggings that were knee-high to match my black knee-high boots, I made sure there was no heel on my boots as I have two pairs of the same boots although one of them has a big heel, whilst the other is flat.

After getting ready I checked my phone and I had loads of texts from Rosie saying how excited she was to come to mine and I was so excited too, so I was going to reply when suddenly I got a call from Bloom. She was screaming down the phone with excitement "Oh my gosh Bloom! Today's the day I can't wait! Are you still coming with me? Please say you are?" I had a split second in my head when I wanted to just say "no sorry change of plans, Rosie is coming over." But I can never be that mean to Ella, so I replied with the same amount of enthusiasm; "Yes, of course, I am coming I wouldn't miss this for the world! I am one of your best mates I want you to be happy!" we then arranged to meet in the biggest shop in the whole mall, near the shoes in Selfridges. Ella said it wasn't very fancy and was a bit boring but I don't think so, do you?

Anyway...

I was finally ready and was so excited then looked at the time, I was nearly 10 minutes late leaving the house so I quickly said goodbyes to my parents and ran out the door. I ran to the met stop and got on the first met that came, once on the met I used their Wi-Fi and checked my messages to see if Rosie understood what time I was picking her up and if she was okay with me being a little late. I got so wrapped up in texting Rosie I didn't notice I had missed my stop, I looked up and we had just left the stop near Ella's house. I got off and the next stop and ran all the way to Ella's.

I knocked on Ella's door and went straight in, she didn't seem to care that I was late instead she was pacing about. I didn't know if she was nervous or very excited so I left her to rant.

I decided that I couldn't listen to her doubting herself so much and wanted to hurry up so that we can go to the mall, then I can go home so I decided to interrupt her and say; "If he doesn't like you then why would he be meeting you? It is not about the image it is mostly about your personality and who you are not what you look like. Trust me you're pretty and gorgeous; If I was a boy I know you would be on my "who to date list" since your kind, honest and an all-around nutter. Any boy would be blind not to notice your beauty and a normal boy would be jealous of any boy on your arm."

I didn't want to sound rude or be mean, so I also made a few jokes, and I wasn't lying either, everything I said came from my heart. Once I had finished the rant she looked at me speechless, mouth half open, so I went over to her and pushed her jaw up and said, "Let's go, put your jacket on and we can get the first bus that comes, and we can get there quicker." She put her denim jacket on and we rushed to the bus stop, we checked the times against our watch and saw it won't come for another 20 minutes...Could the day get any worse?

Ella messaged Shaun about the bus situation so he would understand, he then replied saying that he was in fact stuck in traffic so wouldn't be at the mall any sooner than us. To me this was the worse news I could hear, he lives close to Rosie so if he's stuck in traffic that means that I would be in traffic on the way to pick Rosie. I felt so awful, I wanted to just go home.

With my mind being anywhere but at the bus stop, it felt like forever till the bus turned up, during that time I would just make up random conversations about anything that came to my head so that time could pass quickly, and it worked we got on the bus and made our way to the mall.

I won't go into detail about what happened at the mall because Ella has told you about me walking in the wrong direction, but in my defense, I was mentally in my room sat on my bed trying to sleep.

To put it quickly in a little paragraph, Ella met Shaun and they both ran over to each other and hugged and honestly it was the cutest thing I had ever seen. I felt that I wish I had someone to come over to me and give me a hug and be in a cute relationship. As I have stated before when I am in an uncomfortable moment I start to laugh so I walked over and laughed and randomly said "Ella what do you want to do today?" and they both looked at me and rolled their eyes. I smiled and said; "What? I'm hungry."

Chapter 12: Rush to Rosie.

We walked around doing nothing, I needed to go if we carried on doing nothing as Rosie would be ready now to come mine, I was on the verge of just calling my dad to come pick me up when Ella asked if we want to go to a café and I ran as my little legs could take me to the nearest café. I decided to get them all the same drink as me and looked over and Shaun was whispering into Ella's ear. I honestly didn't care what they were doing at this point, I just wanted to get the drinks and then leave.

Once I put down the Frappuccino's I looked at Ella and she looked at me like she wanted to tell me something but the words weren't coming out of her mouth. I put the straw in my mouth and started drinking, after about 5 minutes we all looked bored again so I took Shaun's phone and started taking selfies, he then gave me a death stare so I started running around away, this cheered everyone up, we were all laughing and getting stitches from it.

"Hey, guys! When you think about it, I could go away now and leave you two, since you are getting on so well." I suggested this to make Bloom think that I was on about her having a romantic moment with Shaun when in reality I wanted to go off, go to the toilet and just cry. I was in a state of sudden panic, it was like the walls were closing in on me and I had no control over what my body was doing and how I felt. I know it sounds sudden but if you read back on the event's I was scared and nervous about how my meeting with Rosie would go, and now I feel late and like it will get too late that my dad won't take me to pick Rosie up. I calmed down eventually, washed my face, went to boots and redid all my makeup with the samples, casually got kicked out of boots then walked back to Ella. As soon as I got back Shaun's mum called him and asked him to meet her when she dropped him off, so we all walked back.

Ella asked to use my phone to call Shaun and talk to him whilst he was in the car on the way home whilst we walked to the bus stop, the bus would be another 40 minutes so I convinced Ella to hang up and finish the conversation, so I could call my dad to pick us up at the mall.

"Dad, the bus isn't for another 40 minutes and I know we have a lot to do tonight so do you think you could pick us up?" I asked in one of those innocent baby voices, making me sound as sweet as possible. He agreed and came and picked me and Ella up.

Chapter 13: Such a Rosie day.

We dropped Ella off and said our goodbyes, and before we could reach the end of her road I was on the phone to Rosie. "I am on my way, just dropped Ella off, I am so sorry we are so late." She forgave me and said she had to go because she was still packing and had to change out of her pajamas, she had a pajama day in with her mum and watched films, which I found very cute because I love having pajama days. That saved me having another panic attack, in my head, I thought she was already ready and giving up waiting for us to come and see her.

For the whole car ride, my dad was singing along to really out of date music, I believe it was from the 1980's but he swore it was from this year... Right okay, dad whatever you want to believe. I started falling asleep because I felt like the car journey was dragging but suddenly got woken up by my dad, he was shouting; "Bloom, we are here. Call Rosie and tell her to come out so I can go and speak to her parents and know exactly where she lives." So I then immediately called Rosie; "Rosie we are outside, come out we are here!" I was so excited. Rosie hung up the phone straight away and ran outside, I leaped out of the car and ran to hug her. I held onto her so tight I was finally spending some time with my new best friend. As we were hugging my dad went to speak to Rosie's parents, introduced himself and then what the plan was for that night and if they wanted to pick Rosie up around lunchtime the next day.

"Rosie I am so excited I have everything planned, we can have a relaxed pamper night. I know you don't like makeup but we can also do whatever you have planned as well." We both started to laugh as I still hadn't stopped hugging her so she replied; "Bloom you are definitely my boo, I believe we won't get any sleep as I have some YouTube videos that I need to show you and we can have a massive laugh." I agreed and then we walked over to put Rosie's stuff into the car as dad had finished talking to Rosie's parents, shook hands with them and then sat in the driver's seat. Me and Rosie placed ourselves in the back seat and as my dad drove off we waved Rosie's parents goodbye.

For the rest of the journey dad was joking around with Rosie saying some really cheesy daddy jokes, these shall never be repeated.

I felt so embarrassed, so when we finally got to mine I shouted "We are here! I need to show you my room, I made the separate bed especially for you." Jumped out of the car, held Rosie's hand and led her upstairs. This insured that dad would go and get Rosie's stuff and place it on the landing and wait for us to come downstairs and collect it, which we did after I showed my room off.

"Bloom I need to tell you something," Rosie said whilst walking over to me. I had just sat down on my bed crossed legged, opening YouTube as Rosie wanted to show me some funny videos. She came sat down next to me and turned to say; "I feel that I'm blessed now to have a friend like you, you see all my friends at school left me, they told me they thought I wasn't a good friend and left." She started to cry, it was like rain pouring from her eyes, I was speechless, I just lent forward and hugged her. No one spoke a word.

"Rosie…I don't know what to say…I will never leave you, you know too much about me. Even my big secret." She moved back and put a smirk on her face and asked, "what secret?" I just laughed. We stayed up gossiping and then she asked to do my hair, no one ever touches my hair, I hardly ever go to the hairdressers as it makes me feel uncomfortable, but I felt I could trust her.

I was right to trust her, she did my hair in two French plaits and she did it so gently that I could feel her braiding each strand of hair, it was amazing.
We started to get tired but still wanted to cherish every moment, so we quickly changed into our pajamas, brushed teeth and went into my bed, under my covers and watched more YouTube videos. I am not sure when, but we fell asleep. I woke up to a YouTube video on talking about how to do ghost makeup look, still not sure why but YouTube is strange like that.

The next day we had chocolate pancakes for breakfast, my dad makes the most amazing ones, not even exaggerating even Rosie, who shall I say is the pickiest eater ever loves them. Once we had finished dad was like; "would you girls like to go to the mall today? I will give you my card and you can buy yourselves each one outfit then meet me for lunch, what do you think?" I turned to Rosie and she turned to me and we both grinned and shouted "Yes!"

We quickly ran upstairs got changed and ran back down. "Ready!" I screamed at the top of my lungs to my dad's face and he just laughed and opened the door.

I was kind of surprised he was allowing me and Rosie to go to the mall in the first place, he usually only lets me go to the mall once a week or even one a month let alone twice in one week, but I wasn't going to argue because he may say that I can't buy an outfit.
Rosie was so excited that when we got to the mall she walked off, it was like she completely forgot I existed, but it was okay as she walked back to find me and gave me a hug and said, "Sorry I was just so excited, is there a shoe shop?" I said yes and told her to wait for a second, said goodbye to my dad and we went looking for the shoe shop.

We went in all of the shops and decided on the outfits we wanted, I got a pale blue crop top, ripped black jeans and a pair of trainers with a French flag on the side. Rosie was harder to shop with, she has a certain style so when she finally picked her outfit it was so her. She decided on a lovely baggy jumper that had a big pocket at the front, light blue jeans with rips in (of course) and sparkly boots which had the most amazing glitter effect on them.

We took the shopping to the food court and sat down and waited for my dad, who when I texted him said he would only be a few minutes he was just in a little traffic. "Bloom, will I ever get to meet some of your friends soon?" Rosie asked looking over at me, I had no idea how to reply or tell her that they don't know anything about her. I just stared blankly at her and saw her looking confused. "Rosie the thing is, they don't really know anything about you, but if you would like we could take a selfie right now and post it to snapchat, this is so they can get an idea of who you are." So we sat there and took tons of selfies and no matter how bad they were they went straight onto snapchat. Within a matter of seconds, I had a message from Ella saying; "Bloom do you have something to tell me? Who is Rosie? Why is she on your snapchat? Answer me, Bloom!"

I don't feel bad for what I did next, and I feel like I shouldn't feel bad, so what I did was just plain blank her and not reply. I did this as I was with Rosie and didn't want to be messaging other people as that can be classed as rude, also If she wanted to start an argument it would be better to have an argument later when Rosie would be gone.

Sadly, I couldn't hide my emotions from Rosie, she knew instantly once I got the message that something was up. She came close to me held my hand and asked; "Bloom are you okay? I know something is up what is wrong?" I just started crying and wouldn't stop.

Suddenly my dad came over and saw me crying and wondered what had happened, Rosie spoke for me and said; "She just had a little argument with her friend, it's nothing really." Dad nodded and walked us to the car and said; "Rosie I have your stuff in the car I think it's time you go home now, we will stop at McDonald's on the way to yours though for tea as you spent so much time shopping you missed out on lunch." We all started to laugh and drove Rossie home. I had school the next day and was so nervous because not only would they be asking Ella about Shaun they may even start asking me about Rosie.

As soon as I got home I ran upstairs called Ella expecting to tell her everything, but I couldn't tell her my secret, so I lied. "Hi Ella, look I am terribly sorry, I didn't want to hurt you it's just… Well, I met Rosie whilst shopping and we got talking and we became friends I am sorry." All I heard was Ella laughing and she took a deep breath and said; "I'm not mad Bloom, I just wondered if you met a random person whilst shopping and became friends, and honestly I am not surprised, you are very open." We spoke nonstop until I fell asleep and so did she.

Chapter 14: School, good old school.

I didn't mind the thought of going to school, now that Ella knew about Rosie I wasn't scared of anything, so I got ready, did all my hair, makeup, that one piece of homework I leave to the last minute then left.

As soon as I got in it happened, everyone coming up to me asking questions about who Shaun was, how they met and if he was a nice guy. I couldn't take it and just walked off to find Ella.

Once I found Ella I was shaking and telling her what had happened and what people were asking me, I didn't know how to reply. She froze, her facial expression changed, she looked really angry, upset and like she wanted to explode. Then out of nowhere, she shouted; "If they want to know what happened so badly, they can come and ask me in person, not through a messenger, because realistically it is none of their business what has happened really, is it?" I didn't know what to say so I started to shake and cry, Ella has never shouted at me like this before, she is always so calm and respectful of everyone, she noticed I was upset and apologized, I understand what she meant when she blamed the pressures of school for why she was so angry. I needed a moment to calm down, so I ran off into the toilet. What if more people come over to me and ask questions about Rosie? They couldn't possibly do that, could they? All these questions spiraled around my head, I just didn't know how to function, so I just stayed in the toilets. After a moment of breathing, I decided to pull out my phone and messaged Rosie about how I was feeling. She was also in school so wouldn't reply, I decided if I write how I am feeling down and vent then it will help me calm down, and so that's what I did then send it to Rosie I felt so much better.

I decided my anxiety was too high for me to go to science, so I decided to put myself into the isolation room with my head of year, she was my favorite teacher, every time I did something or didn't feel right I would go to her and tell her what was up, and she would help. Once I got to her room I immediately broke into tears. "So everyone's coming up to me asking questions." I finished telling her what happened before school, and she agreed for me to stay here. As I am always in her room she had a special cupboard full of hot chocolate, sweets, and cream for me to have whenever I come up to her room. I spent the time drawing in my books and looking over some work I may have missed until I realized that it was nearly break, I asked my head of house if I could go on break early, she allowed me to and said; "If you do ever need me my doors always open, just walk in." Then I left, because I was early I got to choose where I wanted to sit, I saw the table at the end of the hall near a corner, so I decided why not and sat there. Once I had sat down a girl I had never seen before comes over and starts asking; "Your Rosie's friend, right? Well, you should stop she is an idiot and doesn't deserve you in her life." That got to me, so I started to shout, "Don't you say that about her! Plus, you know nothing about me nor about who I should be friends with. She is probably a better friend than you, plus I don't even know you." I was so angry I had no idea where this energy came from, but I was not in control it kept bubbling.

Eventually, she walked away in a huff after I had shouted right at her face. I felt so bad, I had never done something like that, I would never hurt someone's feelings on purpose.

The bell for break chimed and suddenly I saw Ella walking towards me, her face looking so worried that when she saw me she put her arm around me and asked; "Bloom are you okay?" I couldn't open my mouth to speak, the words wouldn't come out but thankfully Linsey, (mine and Ella's friend who spreads gossip,) came over. She was asking me questions, asking if I was okay and if I needed water and what happened to make me look upset, Ella wasn't having any of it though, she told her to go have a bath, that made me smile and have a little laugh. I eventually calmed down and told bloom how I couldn't keep in the secret about Shaun, basically lying to her because Rosie is still new to the situation and I don't want Ella to think she is a bad egg. I do hate lying and would never lie unless it was important, and Rosie is important to me.

After I told Ella the biggest lie ever she hugged me. I kind of let her hug me because she is still one of my closest best friends, although she did make me feel bad for lying when she said; "Bloom, just remember that whatever happens, we will be there for each other. But now I need you to do a massive favor for me."

What is this favor? Does she secretly know what happened and want me to do a favor by not lying? I was scared but I had to say yes.

Luckily, she was asking me to stay by her side and not leave her, till she finally admits to everyone how she and Shaun really met, I understood how she was feeling as when me and Rosie come out, I would want her to stay by my side. I went to hug and placed my face next to her ear and whispered; "We are together forever and always I will never leave you to be on your own. Even if we fall out and completely hate each other, I will never tell anyone what actually happened that night!" This was the only truth I whispered to her that day.

Chapter 15 Doubts.

I decided that me and Ella need to get closer, I could face lying to her again, and the only way to do that is to tell her what she wants to know and have no questions asked.

We ended up planning a movie night, this is when me, Ella and Shaun go see a movie, every week. The last movie I remember seeing was the movie, 'Fifty Shades of Grey.' We saw it come up as an option for a film we could go and see and we all agreed it would be a bit of fun, so we went to see it.

I was so freaked out, I even asked Ella why I said I would go and see this, I had no clue what was going on, but Ella didn't answer Shaun did comically "we are coming up to the best part!" We knew Shaun had never seen this nor did he know what was coming up so we all just ended up laughing at him. Finally, after 2 hours of me hiding my eyes, the movie had finished and Shaun asked Ella, "Can I ask you a question, it is kind of important." He then looked over at me, winked so I told them both I needed the toilet, I knew what was going on and Ella expected nothing.

I went to the bathroom and messaged Rosie what was going on, the message went a bit like this; 'Rosie, Shaun's asking Ella to officially be his girlfriend with a promise ring.' How did I know this was happening? Well, it was about a week or two ago I got a call from Shaun...

"Right Bloom, I would love you to go and try and find out Ella's ring size. Trust me it will be hard, but can you keep it a secret?" (Not like I was keeping loads of secrets from Ella anyway.) I replied with; "Yes I will try, but what's it for can I ask?" Shaun then went on about how much he loves Ella and believes she is the one, I swear I have never cringed so much during a conversation than I did in the 5 minutes he was on the phone to me for. It ended with me saying I would make an excuse that I have to find an average ring size between people for a science experiment.

The next day at school I rushed over to Ella screaming, "OMG Ella what is your ring size? I need to know for.... errrmmm.... a science experiment?" Why was I so bad at lying? Although she did believe me and ask us to go to the ring shop which was only about a 2-minute walk away from our school. Once the final bell rang at school we rushed over to the shop and looked at all the different types of rings, at the end of the day we are still children so we decided we needed to try on every single type of ring there was in that shop that day.

I still never forgot why we were there and made sure I remembered what ring size the assistant told me Ella was. She was a sweet assistant who looked like she was about in her 20s, we had a laugh and then asked her to measure our fingers, I will never forget what she said once we asked, "Sure, as long as none of you two are getting married, you look too young!"- it just made me laugh and stuck in my head ever since. She said this in a jokey way, so we just looked at her with a confused expression, expecting her to say something else but thankfully she didn't. We found out our ring sizes. We spoke about the different rings then decided that maybe one day we would go back there, when we really are getting married to try on wedding rings again, and then make sure it would be even more memorable. I kept checking that Ella wasn't looking then texting what rings she liked the look of, then sending quick pictures of them to Shaun to which, he replied "OK. Ask her what ring size she is?"

On average we spent an hour in that ring shop and every second I made sure I documented for Ella.

After Shaun presented the ring to Ella she was in tears, I made sure I was away whilst this was happening because I am always awkward in romantic situations. My phone suddenly buzzed it was Rosie messaging me, "What happened? Did she say yes? Update me now!" I just laughed at my phone and went back to where Ella and Shaun were. As I was approaching I saw them hugging and the Ring on Ella's left finger and I couldn't help to have a little giggle to myself, Shaun whispered into Ella's ear and she looked at me and grinned and ran to show me the ring.

I told Ella how much I loved it and told them I had to go, this was because I promised Rosie I would skype her about what happened and what Ella said to Shaun. I went to where my dad was picking me up and noticed I had loads of texts from Rosie. I never get this many messages at once if I don't reply, I had no clue what was happening and needed to check ASAP. When in dads car I called Rosie; "Hi, is everything okay what is wrong?" There was silence, then suddenly just loads of crying, I had no clue what to do or say. I just waited. After around 3 minutes she replied; "Bloom, it's just I care about you and heard about what happened at school, just know that I think I'm bad, you shouldn't be friends with someone with this much baggage, just leave me." Before she could put the phone down on me I started shouting, I didn't care that I was sat next to my dad, he wouldn't mind. "Rosie, I love you, you are the best friend I could ask for, you are always there when I'm having a massive meltdown at 1 o'clock in the morning. I couldn't ask for someone better to be here and know all my secrets. So, what if we have haters, everyone does and they are probably just jealous of our friendships that's all." We just ended up crying after I finished speaking, there were no dry eyes anywhere even my dad had to wipe a tear from his face. We spoke till I got home about all that day's events and how no matter what happens we would still be best friends.

Once I got in I hung up the phone and started to get ready for bed, when I get in I always go straight for my pj's as I like to feel cozy, suddenly my phone started ringing, it couldn't be Rosie, I had just hung up the phone on her, so I was really confused, I looked at the caller ID and it was Ella so I answered; "Hello?"

"Oh my gosh Bloom it was the best day ever! When can we do something like this again?"
There was a pause...
"Ella, I think it is best if you go and see him on your own next time."
I couldn't go with her every time she went out with Shaun, I would be a big burden and to be honest I want to spend more time with Rosie, after hearing Rosie having so many doubts about our friendship I felt like she needed the motivation to go out with me and see that no matter what we would be best friends.

Chapter 16: Arguments.

Ella didn't see Shaun for a long time after that day, but me and Rosie saw each other more, we had more sleepovers and we took more selfies than we should have ever taken. You know what though? We didn't care. We were having fun and that was the only thing that mattered. Like all friendships, we all have arguments and mine and Rosie's was when I went to see Shaun with Ella, can you guess why?

Let me begin…

The morning of when I was going with Ella to see Shaun I messaged Rosie, "I'm going to see Shaun today with Ella. If you need me don't hesitate to ring me I will answer." I had no reply, I decided not to worry because she might have been still asleep, or she may have even just misplaced her phone, either way, I didn't worry.
I got ready and decided to order mine and Ella's tickets online so that we could straight away pick them up when we got to the station this would save time.

As we got to the station we saw our train was due in 5 minutes, so we got our tickets out of the machine and ran to the platform, I was so excited that I kept laughing and moving about, I physically couldn't stay still and because of this the cabin crew got so annoyed they moved me and Ella to first class, in a way it didn't feel like a punishment more like an achievement. It was so comfy to sit in first class.

When we got to where Shaun lived we were an hour early, I was still a little hungry as it had been a couple of hours since breakfast so I decided to go to the supermarket and get some doughnuts. Ella thought this was really stupid but I didn't see anything wrong with it (at first.)

When we got to the supermarket I noticed it looked very similar to the one back at home so I knew where the bakery part was without asking, it was kind of a talent of mine. I decided to get chocolate sauce and doughnuts which writing it down does make it sound very stupid, Ella got herself some strawberry drink and a small packet of biscuits, she did this because she wanted to make sure she can eat it in little bites so she can save some for after the meeting, in a way it does sound very smart compared to me.

It was about a 15-minute walk, on average to where Shaun's' school was and when I got there I was really hungry, so I decided to open the packet of doughnuts and eat them there. Whilst eating I heard someone shout; "Who are those two?" I just froze, like who is this person asking who I am, the question should have been who he is and why he needs to know who I am. That whole day I kept checking my phone to see if Rosie had messaged me, she hadn't so I kept worrying, plus I had that Isaac person glaring at me and making me feel really uneasy so, in the end, I whispered into Ella's ear; "Please get Shaun to get rid of Isaac he is making me feel like I've done something wrong, all he is doing is glaring. Can we go?" As soon as I said that Ella nodded and made up a lie in her head to lie to Shaun, she couldn't say in front of his best mate that we didn't like the best mate and wanted to go home, instead she said that our train was due and we needed to go home right that second.

We left and went home, it was probably the worse meet up we have ever encountered and would never want to repeat again.

As soon as I got home I called Rosie, I had to know why she didn't message me that whole day and if anything was up, and by her response, something was definitely up; "Rosie, how are you? You haven't spoken to me all day is everything okay?" there was a pause then a big sigh, she sounded fed up and then said; "You have no clue what you have done, do you?" I said that I was sorry and if there was anything I could do to make things right, but I was still confused about what I did to hurt her, then she told me and it all became clear.

"Bloom, you hurt me, I know you may not know how or why you did, let me explain. When you messaged me saying that you were seeing Shaun I was heartbroken, you knew I go to Shaun's school and would have canceled all my plans just to see you. You didn't invite me."

She was right, I knew all that and still didn't invite her. I was the worse friend ever.

We spoke for hours that night, we spoke about how we felt and what we should do to make it right. I said I was sorry and for her to please forgive me, I had forgotten she went to the school at the time. The argument ended the next morning, we forgave each other and fell asleep, we couldn't fall asleep angry it just wouldn't be right.

Chapter 17: The secret shall remain a secret.

I woke up the next morning feeling very refreshed and like I understood Rosie more now than ever before, I promised on my life and all my loved ones, that I would never betray her like that again.

Although whilst being on the phone to Rosie, Shaun was messaging me worried about Ella, this made me worry too because he kept saying she wasn't answering the phone which is very strange as she would always pick up, so I decided whilst I was getting ready that I should message and call Ella.

She wasn't answering.

I called again, again and again, but still no answer, this was very strange she would not pick up, this made it a mission for me to go to her house and seek the answer out for myself. Whilst on the way to Blooms I decided to call Ella for the final time and she answered. I had been worrying for so long I felt like I was on the verge of tears, I dunno what I would have done if something major had actually happened to her. As soon as she picked up I immediately started to speak; "Oh my gosh Ella, Shaun messaged me last night asking how you were doing and why you weren't answering the phone. I then said you might have just fallen asleep, but he then started saying you blamed me for us going early and I was confused can you explain?" I started to cry after saying this, she didn't speak there was no reply just a sudden silence then she hung up. What just happened? I had no clue what to do but luckily I was just outside her house, I ran up to the door and was banging like crazy shouting for her to answer the door. It felt like hours till the door opened and I was face to face with her ready for answers.

I was drenched from head to foot because when I set off to see Ella I had forgot to pick my coat up and it started to rain, I couldn't go back I knew she needed me so the rain was the least of my worry's. I stepped into the house and just stared at her. She was shaking. I knew she needed a hug and I really wanted to give her one but answers.

Then it finally came to me, she didn't need to tell me what was wrong I needed to tell her. When I was on the phone last night to Rosie a sudden notification came up from Shaun, he had posted a post about Ella, I thought they had made up so I looked at it and saw that it looked strange, I then read it, it explained everything. It said how they met and why he loves her. Why could he do such a mean thing to Ella? He knew she didn't want everyone to know yet he still did it.

I looked Ella in the eyes, placed my hands on her arms and explained; "Ella I'm sorry, everyone at school knows how you met Shaun. Last night when your phone was off Shaun was posting about how much he loves you and he posted this." I unlocked my phone and showed her the Instagram, she was so shocked, she sat down with her hand on her mouth, flooding her face with tears. She was speechless, I asked her what she would like me to do, I felt I needed to do something, anything to make her happy again.

She sighed and said; "I don't know even what I can do now, I might just go in, ignore everyone then go home again." I knew she was serious, today would be a big day, her secret is out before she even had time to hide it, I would hate for mine to be out like that.

She went into school, I held onto her arm between each lesson and every lesson we were in I made sure I sat next to her. It was stressful I kept hearing everyone asking her about the website and calling her an attention seeker, but what could I do, she didn't want me to say anything, so I would show her I was by her side physically.

She walked home alone, didn't allow me to walk to the end of her road like I did every day, instead she made sure I went straight home, I wanted to be with her during this time, as I promised I would do months back and I never break a promise.

As soon as I got home I went on my phone to see if Ella had messaged me, but she didn't someone else had. Rosie. She messaged me saying she couldn't be friends with me anymore, she had wanted to tell me a big secret about how she felt but she couldn't, she felt like she couldn't trust me to be with her anymore. She believed as soon as I know the secret, I would tell everyone. This wasn't the case, I would never tell anyone anything about Rosie, so I called her; "Rosie what is happening? You know I would never leave you or tell anyone what is going on. We have had this conversation before. Please tell me what is up and what I can do to help. I love you." She was quiet, I kept hearing her trying to hold back the tears, but even I couldn't keep back mine. She finally replied; "If I tell you my secret, you have to tell me all of yours. I know I can trust you, I just don't have the confidence to try. Please promise on your life you won't tell a soul." I promised I couldn't tell a soul what the secret was. This means you guys too.

After crying for what felt like days we spoke about everything and sorted it all out, what I didn't notice was that whilst I was on the phone Ella had been trying to contact me with what was happening in her life. She suddenly got extremely worried about why I wasn't answering the phone and if I had done anything.

She called me again 10 minutes later and luckily, I had just got off the phone with Rosie as she went to take a shower. I picked up and said "Hi." Suddenly I had Ella screaming down the phone telling me how worried she was about me and how sorry she was for that day, but she suddenly stopped being sorry and was asking what had happened and why I was in tears. I had to tell her about mine and Rosie's argument, but I didn't know how without spilling the secret, that I had a hunch she already knew. In the end, I said; "It isn't you, just me and Rosie... Never mind you won't know what I am on about."

The way I knew she had a hunch about the secret already is the fact she told me she already knew about who Rosie is, this in itself told me Ella cared so much about me she looked into who Rosie was. I had to think about what she knew and how much she knew. So I went silent.

In the end after hundreds of "Hello, Bloom." I had to force myself to answer and change the subject at the same time, this ended up with me saying; "Yes she is my best friend from outside school, we had an argument, but it will be fine, how are you feeling after today?"

I heard her sigh and say that everything was okay and that she had worked everything out with Shaun, but this made me think she didn't want the subject to change she wanted to know more about the argument and what was happening now.

Chapter 18: Are we friends?

That night I didn't speak to anyone on the phone, I hung up on Ella after we spoke about what happened at school and how tomorrow would be different. I needed some time to myself, no one else just me and my four walls. I started to feel a little lonely so I put my headphones in and started to feel like I had people around me and dozed off to sleep. I woke up to a messaged from Shaun this was weird because he had been messaging me that day about Ella and seeing how she was, I didn't reply because I believed in myself that if he needed to know how somebody was that he would ask them himself and not me, this is due to the fact I didn't know what was happening but all I knew was that it was his fault and should have been apologizing and not message me. The message I got that woke me up went a little something like this; "Bloom I know that you are upset and that something may be going on in your life but trust me things do get better and a problem shared is a problem halved. You have me and Ella to

talk to if you need to, we are here for you just message us." I looked but didn't reply, I couldn't, I couldn't say what was going on. I didn't really know him anyway.
I left it and put my headphones back in, rested my head on my pillow and started to sing with the music in my room. This calmed me down and let my head drift away from reality and into my own world.

Suddenly I got a call from Ella, in my head I was saying to myself "Oh, what does she want now." This does sound mean but it is like I can't have a minute to myself in my own little world. I answered.

"Hi, Ella, what's up?" I made sure I sounded okay and like nothing was up, this was easy for me as I had just had a lovely afternoon to myself in my room. Although she still somehow noticed that something was up with me, her excuse was; "Bloom I know something is up with you, it wouldn't take you this long to answer the phone. Have you done something that you think I would be mad at? Have you had another argument? Please just tell me I promise you I won't be mad."

I couldn't take this secret any longer I needed to at least tell one person who wasn't in the secret but I couldn't find physical words to say, so I cried.

This made Ella worry even more and say, she was already on her way to mine.

My house has never locked the front door when we are all at home, this is so that when my friends or other people want to come in that have been invited they would just walk in, another reason is that I always lose my front door keys, but that's a story for another day. After about 15 minutes I heard someone walk in, rush up the stairs and quickly run into my bedroom, it was Ella. When she came in, I was on the floor next to my bed crying, I had mine and Rosies conversation open on my phone but I couldn't show Ella, she would find out more than I would like her to know. This made it hard for me to tell her the truth.

She immediately ran over and gave me the biggest hug she has ever given me, this made me feel like I could really trust her. I had to stop this before I blurt out everything that was going on, so I pushed her away.

I walked over to my bed and sat on it, crossed legged and then started to tell her everything.

"Ella come and sit next to me I need to tell you something." I patted the space next me and let her walk over, placed my hands on hers and told her what was happening between me and Rosie. I told her how she is my best friend but can't replace Ella. I told her how I did this as I felt alone and didn't want her to feel like I am telling her all my problems and that she will always remain my best friend. Ella started to have tears falling from her eyes, but she wasn't crying with sadness, she looked happy and told me no matter what she is there, a problem shared is a problem halved. I did lie though, I said Rosie couldn't help me, this was mainly because she was the problem that I was crying and how I haven't told Rosie how I have been feeling recently, this was to make Ella think that she knows more than she does.

I ended my rant saying; "You see Ella my life is way too complicated, but I feel like I should tell you a secret I have been keeping to myself for way too long." I then told her my secret although she did have a little giggle and then told me that she already had figured the secret out a couple of days ago. How? Am I really that obvious?

We spoke late into the night, it was a Friday so there was nothing on the next day for neither me nor Ella. Whilst we were speaking on my bed my dad walked in and asked if Ella wanted a lift home, I interrupted that question and asked if Ella could stay. Dad immediately said yes as Ella was a part of the family anyway.
That was the night the secret built our friendship and kept it strong. The night of "The secret of Ella and Bloom."

Chapter 19 : The secret of Ella and Bloom

The next day Ella asked me a strange question, it was strange because even though she knows who Rosie is, she hasn't really got to know who Rosie is as a person. She asked me; "The thing is I have been thinking about it, what we spoke about last night, and don't really know who Rosie is. Can you please tell me who she is, only if you feel up to it?"

I felt speechless because it was true, she knew of Rosie and knows mine and Rosie's friendship but she doesn't exactly know who Rosie is. I invited Ella to sit next to me and showed her a picture of who Rosie was. She was surprised, it was like Rosie had changed in her opinion. This is when she went home, she told me that if I ever need her she is a phone call away.

I rang Rosie and explained to her what happened that night, she agreed it was right for me to let Ella in, this was mainly because Ella was one of my closest friends and needed to know that I knew what I was doing. This made Rosie agree and then she said, "You do know Ella is on my Facebook right now? My phone has just told me, I just have to laugh." We then laughed and knew that Shaun would start asking questions at school, Rosie is strong enough handle Shaun anyway.

Rosie called me a couple of days later laughing, she said Shaun approached her and wanted to take a selfie to send to Ella, this is all he did which surprised me, I thought he would have had a full interrogation and find out every detail about her. We laughed late into the night and fell asleep on the phone.

This is where I now end the story. I hope you have figured out the secret and don't have that many questions on your mind. Just know that if you have figured the secret out not to tell anyone else because it is mine and Ella's secret.

Hope you enjoyed reading and would want to know more. Until next time my friends.

Bloom xxx

Printed in Great Britain
by Amazon